C000281618

British Library Cataloguing in Publication Data
Southgate, Mark
The fisherman and his wife.
I. Title
823'.914[J] PZ7

ISBN 0-86264-160-8

First published in Great Britain by Andersen Press Ltd.,
62–65 Chandos Place, London WC2.
Published in Australia by Century Hutchinson Australia Pty. Ltd.,
16–22 Church Street, Hawthorn, Victoria 3122.

Colour separated in Switzerland by Photolitho AG Offsetreproduktionen,
Gossau, Zürich.
Printed in Italy by Grafiche AZ, Verona.

The FISHERMAN AND HIS WIFE

Mark Southgate

Andersen Press · London
Hutchinson of Australia

There was once a fisherman who lived with his wife Ilsebill in an old hut.

Early each morning he would walk to the sea and spend his day fishing.

One morning the fisherman caught the biggest fish he had ever seen.

"I am not a real fish but an enchanted prince," cried the fish. "If you spare me, I'll grant you any wish you like."

"I would like a gold coin, please," gasped the fisherman.
Before he could blink, there in his hand was a sparkling coin.

The fisherman ran home and told his wife what had happened.

At first she was happy, but after some thought she said, "I don't think one coin is enough for saving that fish's life. Go back and demand a sackful."

The fisherman ran back to the sea and called out,

> "O man of the sea!
> Come listen to me!
> My wife Ilsebill
> Will have her own will."

As he spoke, the fish returned. "What is it?" he whispered.

"My wife would like a sack of gold, please," replied the fisherman.

There was a flash of lightning and there before him was the sack.

When the fisherman returned to his wife she had changed her mind.

"It's all very well having money," she said, "but look at this dirty old hut we live in. Go and get a new house."

So off the fisherman ran.

When the fisherman reached the shore, the sea looked dark and gloomy. He called to the fish,

> "O man of the sea!
> Come listen to me!
> My wife Ilsebill
> Will have her own will."

"What do you want this time?" sighed the fish.

"My wife would like a house, please," replied the fisherman.

There was another flash of lightning and off he ran.

For a while the fisherman and his wife lived happily in their new house until one day Ilsebill exclaimed, "Why do we live here when we could have a castle? Go and tell the fish I want a castle."

The fisherman ran back to the sea. Dark clouds gathered as he shouted into the wind,

> "O man of the sea!
> Come listen to me!
> My wife Ilsebill
> Will have her own will"

"What do you want now?" muttered the fish.

"She doesn't think the house is grand enough, so she wants a castle," explained the fisherman.

There was another flash of lightning and off he ran, thinking how happy Ilsebill would be with her castle.

But a castle is difficult to clean. “Go back and demand servants,” she ordered the fisherman.

The dark sea crashed angrily against the rocks as the fisherman called to the fish,

> "O man of the sea!
> Come listen to me!
> My wife Ilsebill
> Will have her own will."

"What now?" snapped the fish.

"She is demanding servants," replied the fisherman.

"Go back," said the fish, "and you will find your servants working hard. Your wife should be happy now."

But soon Ilsebill dreamed about greater things. "How nice it would be if I were a powerful queen with an army!" she exclaimed.

So the fisherman went back to the sea. The sky grew black and stormy as the wind lashed the waves into a fury. He called out to the fish,

"O man of the sea!
Come listen to me!
My wife Ilsebill
Will have her own will."

The fish was angry when the fisherman told him of his wife's wish to be a queen.

"Very well," shouted the fish, "but do not disturb me again!"

For many days the queen ordered everyone about, but soon she became bored and summoned the fisherman.

“It’s all very well being queen, but I fancy more power. Go back to the fish and order him to make me God and give me the power to make the sun rise and set,” she said.

When the fisherman reached the shore, he trembled as the storm rattled his bones. His words were nearly lost in the howling wind as he appealed to the fish,

> "O man of the sea!
> Come listen to me!
> My wife Ilsebill
> Will have her own will."

When the fish appeared the fisherman told him that his wife wished to be God and have the power to make the sun rise and set.

"Your wife is greedy!" roared the fish. "If she's not content with what she's got then she'll have nothing!"

Then the fish commanded a great wave to sweep over the land.

When the storm was over, the fisherman and his greedy wife were back in their hut again.